THE USBORNE YOUNG SCIENTIST
UNDERSEA

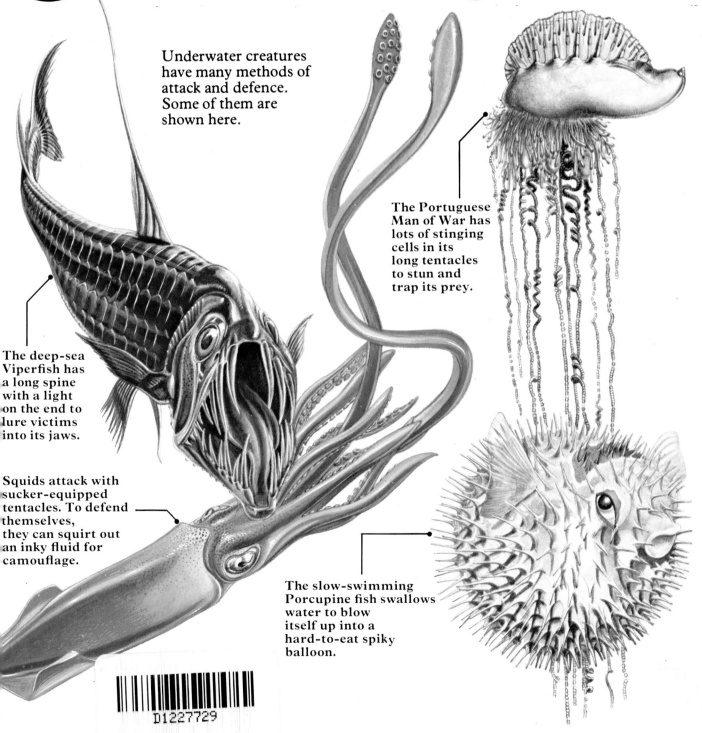

Underwater creatures have many methods of attack and defence. Some of them are shown here.

The Portuguese Man of War has lots of stinging cells in its long tentacles to stun and trap its prey.

The deep-sea Viperfish has a long spine with a light on the end to lure victims into its jaws.

Squids attack with sucker-equipped tentacles. To defend themselves, they can squirt out an inky fluid for camouflage.

The slow-swimming Porcupine fish swallows water to blow itself up into a hard-to-eat spiky balloon.

D1227729

Credits

Written by
Christopher Pick
Art and Editorial direction
David Jefferis
Design Assistant
Iain Ashman

Illustrated by
Malcolm English
Christine Howes
Malcolm McGregor
Michael Roffe
Phil Weare
John Brettoner
Cover illustration by
Philip Hood

Acknowledgements
We wish to thank the following
for their assistance and for
making available material in
their collections.
Alwyne Wheeler
Robin Eccles
British Sub-Aqua Club
DHB Construction Ltd
DG Swales
Grumman Aerospace
Jerry Hazzard
Royal Navy

Buoyancy meter devised by Heather
Amery.
First published in 1977 by Usborne
Publishing Ltd, Usborne House, 83-
85 Saffron Hill, London EC1N 8RT,
England. This edition, copyright ©
1977, 1990 Usborne Publishing Ltd.
Revised and updated 1990. The name
Usborne and the device 🐝 are
trade marks of Usborne Publishing
Ltd. All rights reserved. No part
of this publication may be
reproduced, stored in a retrieval
system, or transmitted in any form
or by any means, electronic,
mechanical, photocopying, recording
or otherwise without prior
permission of the publisher.
Printed in Italy

On the cover: A great white shark

On this page: a diving saucer
cruises over the sea bed

The experiments

Here is a checklist of the equipment you will need for the
experiments and things to do included in this book.

General equipment

Notebook and pencil
Rule or tape-measure
Sticky tape
Glue
Scissors
Salt
Paperclips
Rubber bands

For special experiments

Light and heavy water (p.5):
Glass bowl
Jug
Bottle of coloured ink

Salts in the seas (p.5):
Shallow bowl or saucer
Table salt

Water buoyancy meter (p.17):
Bowl
250 g plasticine
Sheet of thick card 250 mm
× 30 mm
Used match
Three paperclips
Rubber band
Table salt

Underwater corrosion (p.17):
Two baked-bean tin lids
Two iron nails
Bowl
Table salt
Cotton thread

Make your own periscope (p. 20):
Two small hand mirrors
Balsa cement
Sheet of 6 mm thick balsa wood
700 mm × 76 mm
Allow another sheet of 6 mm thick
balsa wood 250 mm × 76 mm
to make the other components
Transparent acetate

The weight of water (p.24):
Two empty ballpoint pen cases
Plasticine
Waterproof sticky tape
Milk bottle
Balloon
Plastic or rubber tubing

Weights and measures

All the weights and measures used in this book are Metric.
This list gives some equivalents in Imperial measures.

mm = millimetre
(1 inch = 25.4 mm)

cm = centimetre
(1 inch = 2.54 cm)

m = metre
(1 yard = 0.91 m)

km = kilometre
(1 mile = 1.6 km)

kph = kilometres per hour
(100 mph = 160 kph)

g = gram
(10 g = 0.353 oz)

kg = kilogram
(1 pound = 0.45 kg)

A tonne is 1,000 kg
(1 ton = 1.02 tonnes)

kg/sq cm = kilograms per
square centimetre
(1 pound per square inch =
0.07 kg/sq cm)

1 litre is 1.76 pints

°C = degrees Centigrade

THE USBORNE YOUNG SCIENTIST
UNDERSEA

About this book

What is a food pyramid? Why do fish have lateral lines? How do submarines dive, steer and surface?

The Undersea answers these questions and many more. It shows the reader how deep-diving machines are now opening up the Earth's last frontier—the world of inner space. It covers developments such as fish farming, mining the ocean floors and new ways to control pollution.

The Undersea also contains safe and simple experiments that can be done at home with ordinary household equipment. They range from projects like building a periscope to demonstrations of the principles of water pressure and buoyancy.

Contents

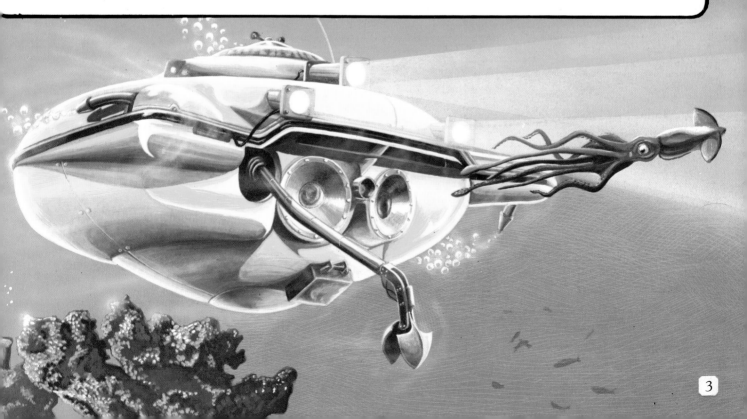

Planet Earth, the water world

The planet we live on, the Earth, has really been misnamed, as you can see from these three views of it—no less than 70.8 per cent of the world is covered in water!

The different parts of the sea have different names, but they are all connected and water flows continually around the world.

Life started in the sea, and although many forms of life live on land, the majority still live in the cradle of life—the sea.

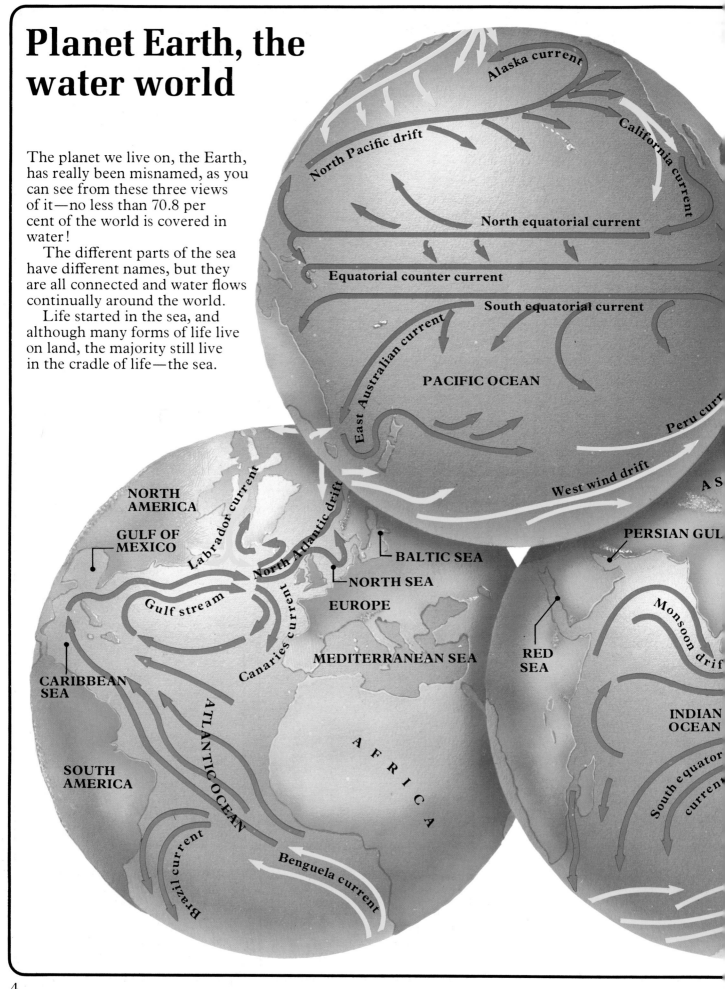

Alaska current
California current
North Pacific drift
North equatorial current
Equatorial counter current
South equatorial current
East Australian current
PACIFIC OCEAN
Peru curr
West wind drift
A S

NORTH AMERICA
GULF OF MEXICO
Labrador current
North Atlantic drift
BALTIC SEA
NORTH SEA
EUROPE
Gulf stream
Canaries current
MEDITERRANEAN SEA
CARIBBEAN SEA
ATLANTIC OCEAN
SOUTH AMERICA
A F R I C A
Brazil current
Benguela current

PERSIAN GUL
Monsoon drif
RED SEA
INDIAN OCEAN
South equator
current

Highways of the Seas

Cold water currents

Warm water currents

Key to currents on globes at left

Ocean currents are the highways of the seas. Cold currents, produced by melting ice, start in the Arctic and Antarctic. Cold water is heavier than warm, so they flow at a great depth. The faster-flowing warm currents, usually starting around the equator, move nearer the surface.

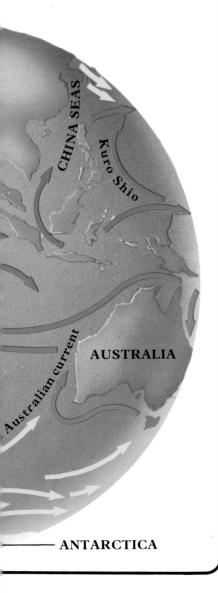

CHINA SEAS

Kuro Shio

Australian current

AUSTRALIA

ANTARCTICA

Light and heavy water

1

HOT WATER

GLASS BOWL

▲ This simple experiment shows you why cold and warm water currents flow at the bottom and top of the seas. You need a glass bowl, a small jug and a bottle of ink. Fill the bowl three-quarters full of cold water.

2

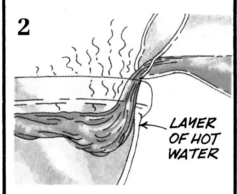

LAYER OF HOT WATER

▲ Fill the jug up with hot (but not boiling) water, and drop some ink in to colour it. Gently pour the hot water into the bowl. You will see that the hot water stays on the surface, forming a definite top layer.

3

WATER MIXES AS IT COOLS

HOT WATER COOLING DOWN

▲ After a while the hot water will cool off and mix with the rest. The reason why hot water stays on top is because water expands when it is heated—this makes it lighter, so it floats on top of the heavier, denser cold water.

Salts in the seas

1

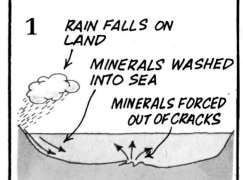

RAIN FALLS ON LAND

MINERALS WASHED INTO SEA

MINERALS FORCED OUT OF CRACKS

▲ Most salts and minerals are washed off the land by rain and carried into the sea by streams and rivers. The salts remain in the sea even when the water evaporates. This experiment shows how the process of evaporation works.

2

SAUCER OR SHALLOW TIN LID

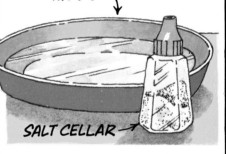

SALT CELLAR

▲ Fill the saucer with water, and put in as much salt as will dissolve—stir with a teaspoon to help if necessary. Put the saucer in a warm, dry place and leave it for a few days. Keep a daily note of the water level.

3

SALT CRYSTALS

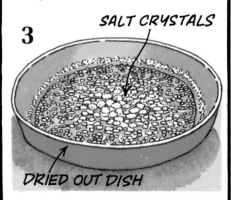

DRIED OUT DISH

▲ You will find the level sinking. The water is gradually turning into vapour—evaporating—and escaping into the atmosphere. It leaves the salt behind (like the salts in the oceans) to leave nothing but large salt crystals.

The living oceans

The sea is not just a flat expanse of water, the same from top to bottom. It varies a lot from place to place. The creatures in the sea, like those on land, have adapted in different ways to the kind of environment in which they live. Deep-sea fish, for example, are equipped with organs to lure prey and big jaws to swallow with.

Studying the undersea, the science of oceanography, is fairly new—the first detailed studies were not made until the 19th century.

▲ The first scientific expedition to explore the undersea sailed in *HMS Challenger* (shown above) in 1872. The scientists on board mapped the ocean floors and collected many specimens of ocean life during the voyage.

A habitat four kilometres deep

The sea is divided into two main parts. The Benthic area is the sea bottom, together with the creatures that live on it. The rest of the ocean is called the Pelagic area and is divided into three zones.

The photic, sunlit, zone at the top receives a lot of sunlight. Many creatures live there, in contrast with the euphotic, twilight zone, where there is little plant life.

Deeper down, there is no light at all, and little food. The inhabitants of the abyss, the sunless zone, are mainly small and well equipped to trap any prey that may come their way.

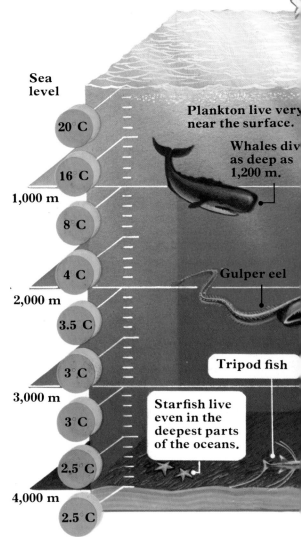

Sea level

20 C

16 C

1,000 m

8 C

4 C

2,000 m

3.5 C

3 C

3,000 m

3 C

2.5 C

4,000 m

2.5 C

Plankton live very near the surface.

Whales dive as deep as 1,200 m.

Gulper eel

Tripod fish

Starfish live even in the deepest parts of the oceans.

Landscape under the sea

The bottom of the sea has a 'landscape' of its own. Off most coasts the land gently slopes out across the continental shelf before falling steeply to the seabed. Nor is the seabed itself flat. There are trenches, canyons and mountain ranges—the tiniest islands are often merely the tips of enormous underwater peaks.

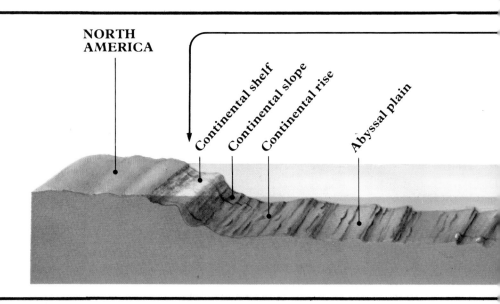

NORTH AMERICA

Continental shelf

Continental slope

Continental rise

Abyssal plain

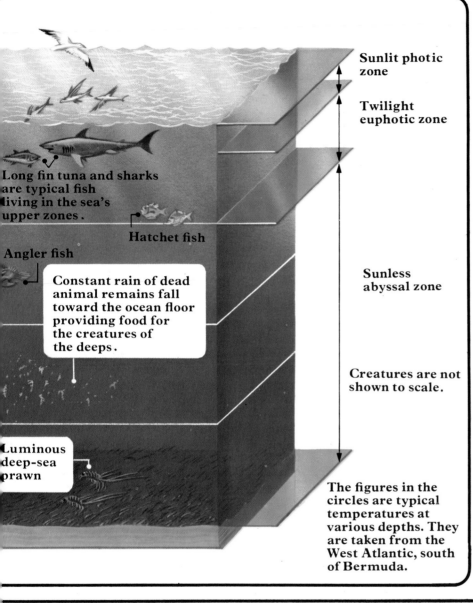

Sunlit photic zone

Twilight euphotic zone

Long fin tuna and sharks are typical fish living in the sea's upper zones.

Hatchet fish

Angler fish

Constant rain of dead animal remains fall toward the ocean floor providing food for the creatures of the deeps.

Sunless abyssal zone

Creatures are not shown to scale.

Luminous deep-sea prawn

The figures in the circles are typical temperatures at various depths. They are taken from the West Atlantic, south of Bermuda.

Food pyramids

The diagram below shows just one example of a food pyramid. 1,000 kg of phytoplankton, tiny plants, will feed 100 kg of zooplankton, animals. These zooplankton will in turn provide enough food for 10 kg of fish such as mackerel, which will sustain 1 kg of killer whale. Because so many small creatures are needed to feed larger ones there are always fewer large animals in the oceans than small ones.

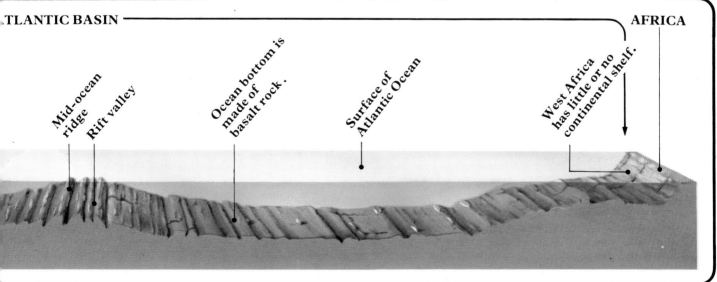

ATLANTIC BASIN

AFRICA

Mid-ocean ridge

Rift valley

Ocean bottom is made of basalt rock.

Surface of Atlantic Ocean

West Africa has little or no continental shelf.

Creatures of the sea

About 20,000 kinds of fish live in the sea. Most have bony skeletons. They are called teleosts after the Greek words which mean 'made of bone'. Others, like rays and sharks have skeletons of gristle. Octopuses and squids (which are not fish, but molluscs) have skeletons of chalky calcium carbonate.

Water

▲ Like people, fish need oxygen, but they get it from water, not air. As a fish swallows, water passes through its gills which 'strain' the oxygen from it. The de-oxygenated water is expelled through the gill covers.

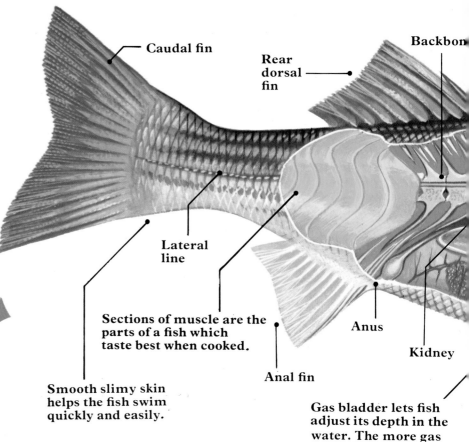

Caudal fin

Rear dorsal fin

Backbon

Lateral line

Sections of muscle are the parts of a fish which taste best when cooked.

Smooth slimy skin helps the fish swim quickly and easily.

Anal fin

Anus

Kidney

Gas bladder lets fish adjust its depth in the water. The more gas in the bladder, the more buoyant the fis

Colour and camouflage

Camouflage is a fish's main protection against attack by a larger fish. Some fish also use camouflage when attacking and blend into the background until they are ready to strike.

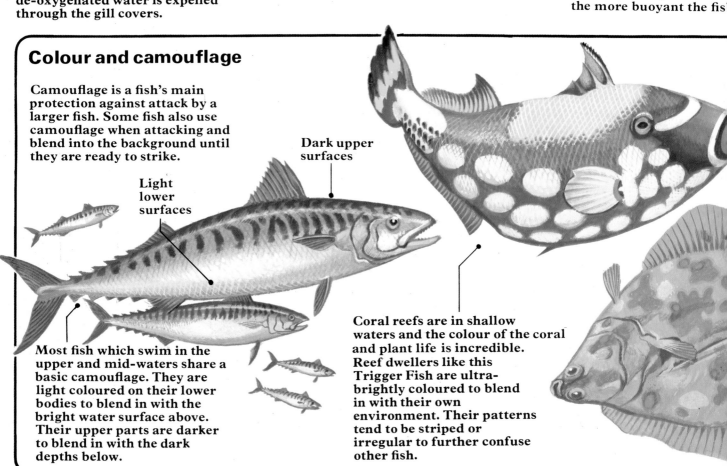

Dark upper surfaces

Light lower surfaces

Most fish which swim in the upper and mid-waters share a basic camouflage. They are light coloured on their lower bodies to blend in with the bright water surface above. Their upper parts are darker to blend in with the dark depths below.

Coral reefs are in shallow waters and the colour of the coral and plant life is incredible. Reef dwellers like this Trigger Fish are ultra-brightly coloured to blend in with their own environment. Their patterns tend to be striped or irregular to further confuse other fish.

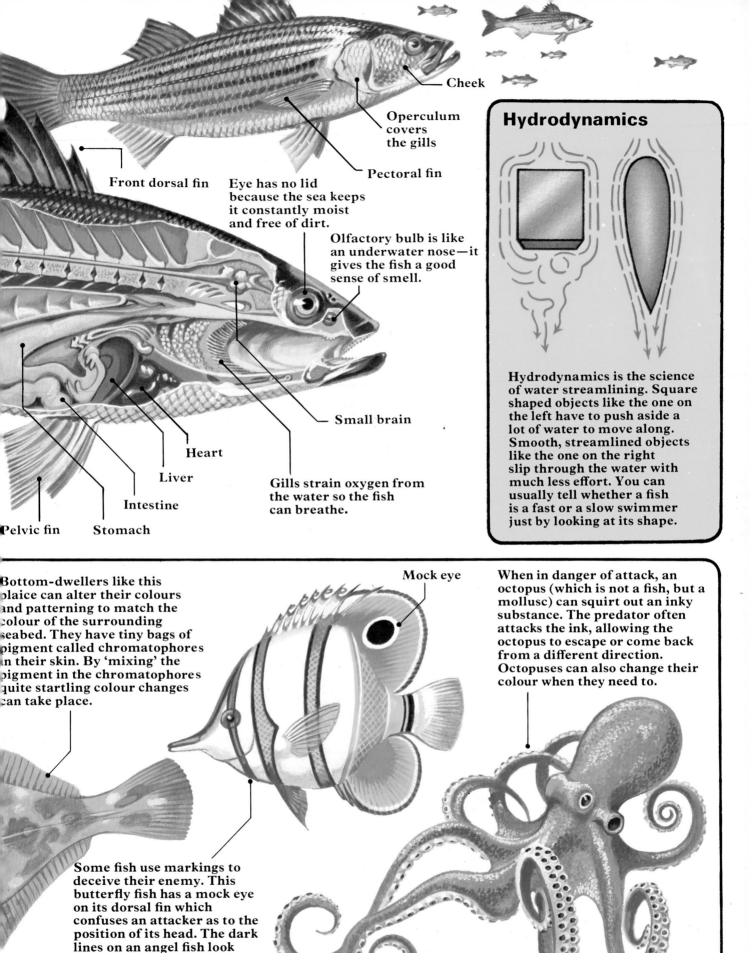

Cheek

Operculum
covers
the gills

Pectoral fin

Front dorsal fin

Eye has no lid
because the sea keeps
it constantly moist
and free of dirt.

Olfactory bulb is like
an underwater nose—it
gives the fish a good
sense of smell.

Small brain

Heart

Liver

Intestine

Gills strain oxygen from
the water so the fish
can breathe.

Pelvic fin   Stomach

Hydrodynamics

Hydrodynamics is the science
of water streamlining. Square
shaped objects like the one on
the left have to push aside a
lot of water to move along.
Smooth, streamlined objects
like the one on the right
slip through the water with
much less effort. You can
usually tell whether a fish
is a fast or a slow swimmer
just by looking at its shape.

Bottom-dwellers like this
plaice can alter their colours
and patterning to match the
colour of the surrounding
seabed. They have tiny bags of
pigment called chromatophores
in their skin. By 'mixing' the
pigment in the chromatophores
quite startling colour changes
can take place.

Mock eye

Some fish use markings to
deceive their enemy. This
butterfly fish has a mock eye
on its dorsal fin which
confuses an attacker as to the
position of its head. The dark
lines on an angel fish look
like the weeds and plants
among which it lives.

When in danger of attack, an
octopus (which is not a fish, but a
mollusc) can squirt out an inky
substance. The predator often
attacks the ink, allowing the
octopus to escape or come back
from a different direction.
Octopuses can also change their
colour when they need to.

Underwater diving

People have explored underwater for many centuries. They used to hold their breath and come up frequently for air. It was not until the invention of SCUBA gear that they had the freedom to swim underwater like fish.

SCUBA – which stands for Self Contained Underwater Breathing Apparatus – was invented by two Frenchmen, Emile Gagnan and Jacques Cousteau. They used the equipment for the first time in June 1943.

Since then, SCUBA, also known as the aqualung, has become popular world-wide.

Water creatures

Humans are very watery creatures. Believe it or not, 73% of your body is made of ordinary water.

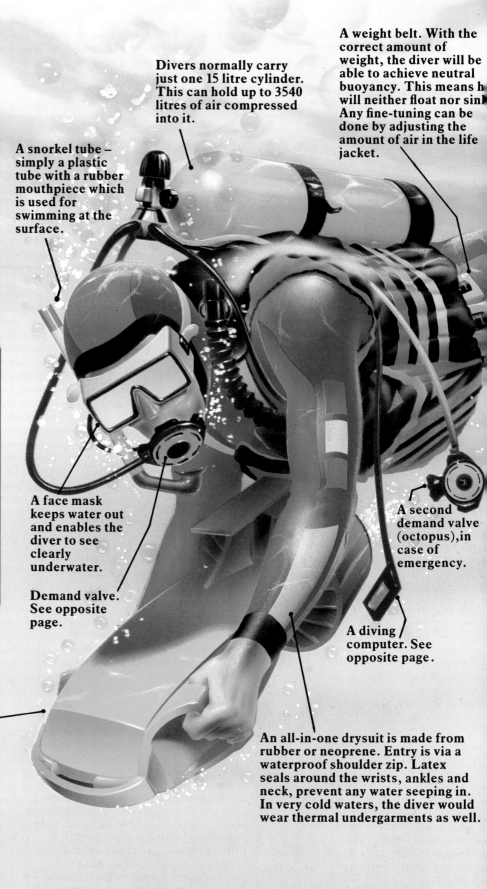

Divers normally carry just one 15 litre cylinder. This can hold up to 3540 litres of air compressed into it.

A weight belt. With the correct amount of weight, the diver will be able to achieve neutral buoyancy. This means h will neither float nor sin Any fine-tuning can be done by adjusting the amount of air in the life jacket.

A snorkel tube – simply a plastic tube with a rubber mouthpiece which is used for swimming at the surface.

A face mask keeps water out and enables the diver to see clearly underwater.

Demand valve. See opposite page.

A second demand valve (octopus),in case of emergency.

A diving computer. See opposite page.

Swimming underwater for long distances can be very tiring and some divers choose to use a diver propulsion vehicle like the one shown here. It is electrically powered and can tow a diver through the water at about three to four kph. It will work down to a depth of 75m.

An all-in-one drysuit is made from rubber or neoprene. Entry is via a waterproof shoulder zip. Latex seals around the wrists, ankles and neck, prevent any water seeping in. In very cold waters, the diver would wear thermal undergarments as well.

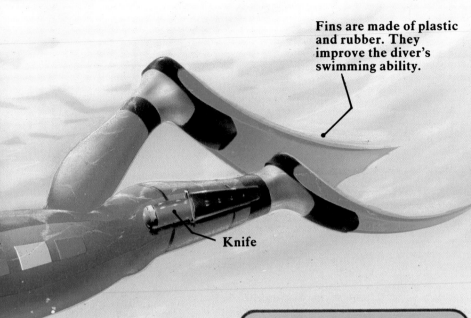

Fins are made of plastic and rubber. They improve the diver's swimming ability.

Knife

Cameras

Flash gun

Waterproof housing

Underwater cameras are both waterproof and robust. Divers can use an ordinary camera protected by a waterproof housing. They need a powerful flash gun to illuminate the picture.

How SCUBA gear works

Demand valve

▲ Divers need a regular supply of air – neither too much nor too little. It must also be at exactly the same pressure as the water in which they are swimming. The demand valve controls both these things.

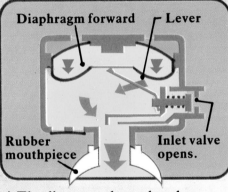

Diaphragm forward — Lever

Rubber mouthpiece

Inlet valve opens.

▲The diagrams above show how the demand valve works. By breathing in, the diaphragm is sucked forward operating the lever and opening the inlet valve. The air flow is then directed to the diver's mouth via the mouthpiece.

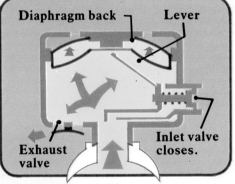

Diaphragm back — Lever

Exhaust valve

Inlet valve closes.

When the diver breathes out, the diaphragm is allowed to fall back into position and the lever pushes the inlet valve closed. Exhaled air passes out into the water via the small one-way exhaust valve.

Diver using a single cylinder

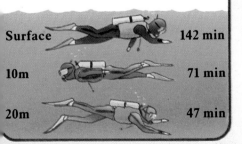

Surface	142 min
10m	71 min
20m	47 min

▲ The deeper a diver goes, the more air is needed to counter-balance the increasing pressure from the surrounding water. The diagram above shows how long a 15 litre cylinder will last at various depths.

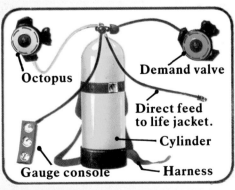

Octopus

Demand valve

Direct feed to life jacket.

Cylinder

Gauge console

Harness

▲ A complete aqua-lung assembly as shown here, is fitted with a 15 litre cylinder, a harness and a number of hoses. The hoses are needed to feed air to the demand valve, octopus, life jacket and gauge console.

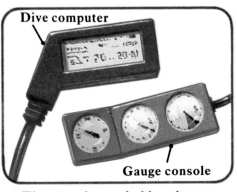

Dive computer

Gauge console

▲ The console may hold such things as a contents gauge, depth gauge, compass, thermometer or timer. Some divers prefer a diving computer which offers all of the above facilities but is often smaller and lighter.

Wrecks and treasures

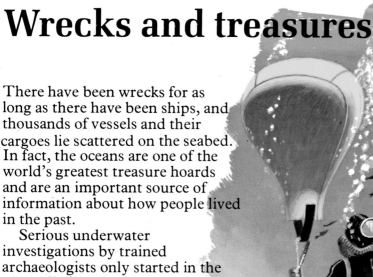

There have been wrecks for as long as there have been ships, and thousands of vessels and their cargoes lie scattered on the seabed. In fact, the oceans are one of the world's greatest treasure hoards and are an important source of information about how people lived in the past.

Serious underwater investigations by trained archaeologists only started in the 1950s. Before then, many wrecks had been looted and spoiled by treasure-seekers interested not in the past but only in the cash they could get for their finds.

▶ This picture shows some of the ways in which underwater archaeologists record and retrieve remains from ocean wrecks. These remains are from an ancient Greek trading boat.

This diver is letting air from his aqualung into an ancient wine jug. Once filled with air, it will rise up to the surface.

This bag catches any valuable items sucked up by the air lift.

Air-filled balloons lift heavy loads from the seabed to the surface. This odd-shaped lump is made of lots of iron fragments rusted together.

Metal detectors like the one this diver is carrying help to locate objects such as coins and jewellery.

Undersea air lift, used to suck up the sand and mud that the current continually deposits on the wreck.

Danger in the deeps

▲ The invention of SCUBA gear meant that divers were able to explore freely in the depths, like the camera-equipped diver above. One danger remained though—the bends—agonizing pains which can cause paralysis or death.

▲ Water pressure will crush a diver's lungs unless the force of his air supply equals it. Under high pressure, the diver breathes more air than normal and the extra nitrogen in the air is absorbed into the diver's body.

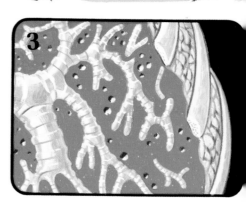

▲ As the diver surfaces, the pressure from the surrounding water decreases. If he comes up too quickly the nitrogen absorbed into his body (lungs are shown in close-up above) will not escape, but will bubble like fizzy lemonade.

his two-man submarine, ecially built for derwater archaeology, the easy way to map t a wreck. Equipped with o cameras, it can go wn as deep as 180 m and n photograph a whole te in only a few hours.

Scaffolding divides up remains into small areas.

A sketch book and pencil is one way of recording a find—but because the artist is underwater, the 'pencil' has to be a graphite crayon and the 'paper' a sheet of plastic.

Two centuries under the sea

Not all wrecks are as well preserved as the Vasa, a ship which was raised intact more than 300 years after she sank in Stockholm harbour in Sweden. Ships usually broke up, either against rocks or as a result of the pounding action of the sea. In these cases, marine archaeologists have to turn detective and scour the seabed over wide areas looking for finds just as they would on land, their work being even more difficult.

▲ The pictures above and right show what could happen to a wreck. Above, the contents are strewn over rocks as the hull is torn open. Right, currents and sand spread and cover the ship's remains.

Hull after sinking 1

100 years later 2

150 years later 3

200 years later 4

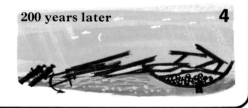

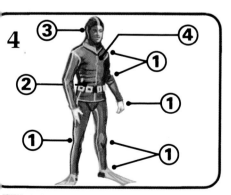

4

▲ Nitrogen bubbles in the body can ave effects like this. In nerves), they cause pains in bones, joints nd muscles. In the spine (2), they ause paralysis. In the brain (3), izzyness and convulsions. In e blood (4), asphyxia and choking.

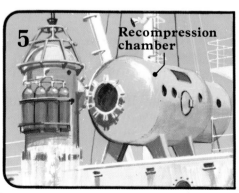

5 **Recompression chamber**

▲ To overcome an attack of the bends, the victim is put into a recompression chamber. Air is pumped in at high pressure and then very slowly released. The diver is brought slowly back to the correct pressure, giving the

6

Depth of dive	Length of dive
10m	232mins
20m	46mins
30m	20mins
40m	11mins
50m	7mins

nitrogen time to escape without forming bubbles. The diagram above shows how long a diver can spend underwater at different depths without risking an attack of the bends and without slowing down his ascent to the surface.

Sharks and rays

Sharks, rays and skate are fish which have no bony skeletons—they are made of gristly cartilage—so they are called cartilaginous fish.

Sharks have no gill covers, so they cannot retain water in their gills. So that they can strain enough oxygen from the water to breathe, they have to keep swimming all the time, so that water is flowing continuously over their gills.

Though only 12 species of shark are classed as man-eaters, the behaviour of all except the harmless whale and basking sharks is utterly unpredictable.

▼ ▶ Sharks are the biggest group of cartilaginous fish and are among the oldest creatures in the ocean. The first sharks lived 350 million years ago and their modern descendants have hardly changed in appearance.

The thresher shark's strongpoint is its tail, which it uses to round-up and stun smaller fish such as mackerel and herring before it devours them.

The whale shark is the gentle giant of the oceans. Though it grows up to 17 m long, it lives off plankton, swims very slowly and is quite harmless. It is the largest fish in the sea.

The hammerhead shark gets its name because of the shape of its head. Its eyes and nostrils are at each end of the hammer.

This SCUBA-equipped diver is shown to the same scale as the sharks.

▲ The manta ray does not live on the bottom like most rays but swims close to the surface. The horns on either side of its mouth guide in water from which it can filter plankton to eat. If it is ever chased, the manta ray can leap out of the water to safety.

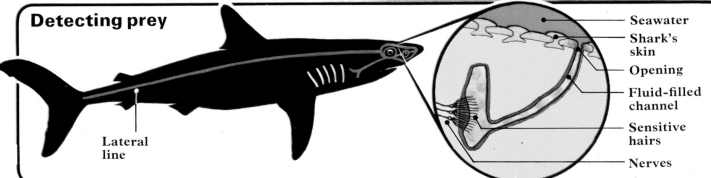

Detecting prey

Lateral line

Seawater
Shark's skin
Opening
Fluid-filled channel
Sensitive hairs
Nerves

▲ Like other fish, sharks have a special system for locating prey called the lateral line. Underneath the lateral line are lots of openings, each at the head of a channel filled with fluid. If a fish moves nearby, the movement of the water presses on the fluid. In turn, this presses on to sensitive hairs at the end of the channel. These are attached to nerve endings linked to the shark's brain.
The system is so sensitive that the shark knows the exact position of its prey and can attack. It even knows, within limits, the health of its prey—wounded fish thrash about, dying fish move much more gently. Both movements are sensed by the lateral line system.

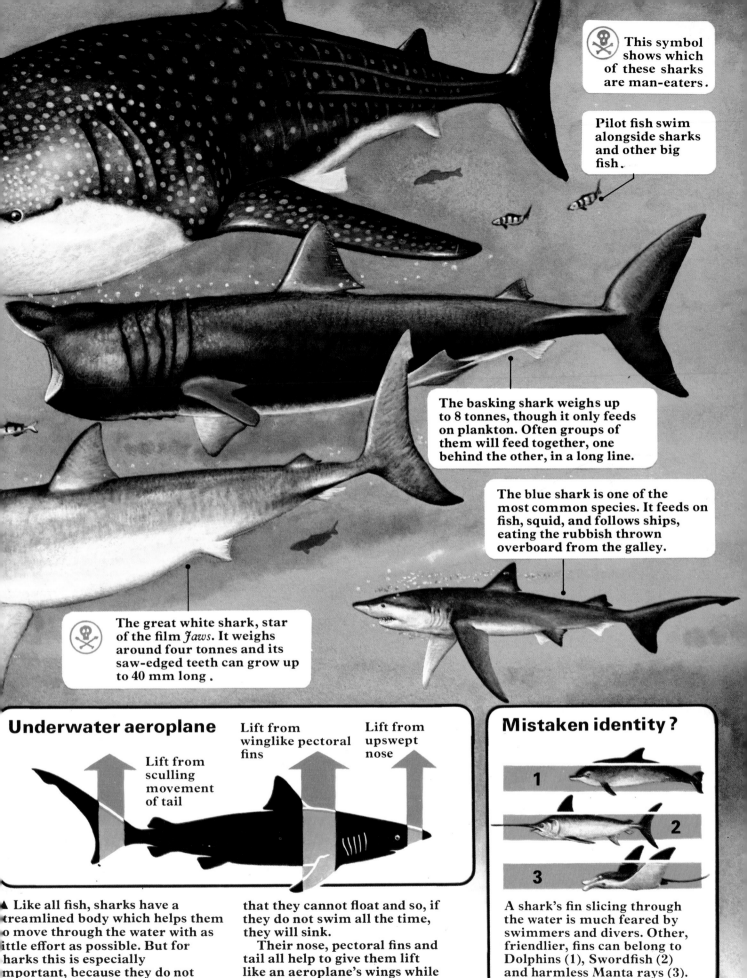

Pilot fish swim alongside sharks and other big fish.

The basking shark weighs up to 8 tonnes, though it only feeds on plankton. Often groups of them will feed together, one behind the other, in a long line.

The blue shark is one of the most common species. It feeds on fish, squid, and follows ships, eating the rubbish thrown overboard from the galley.

The great white shark, star of the film *Jaws*. It weighs around four tonnes and its saw-edged teeth can grow up to 40 mm long.

Underwater aeroplane

Lift from sculling movement of tail

Lift from winglike pectoral fins

Lift from upswept nose

Mistaken identity?

1

2

3

Like all fish, sharks have a streamlined body which helps them to move through the water with as little effort as possible. But for sharks this is especially important, because they do not have a swimbladder. This means that they cannot float and so, if they do not swim all the time, they will sink.

Their nose, pectoral fins and tail all help to give them lift like an aeroplane's wings while they move through the water.

A shark's fin slicing through the water is much feared by swimmers and divers. Other, friendlier, fins can belong to Dolphins (1), Swordfish (2) and harmless Manta rays (3).

Underwater armour

JIM is the nickname for a type of armoured diving suit developed in the 1970s. The air pressure inside it is the same as that of the Earth's atmosphere. This means that most of the problems of working at considerable depths are avoided. Divers can explore down to about 610m and can return to the surface without having to decompress.

Also, there is an example below of a submersible machine in which divers can work at these depths with similar protection.

The JIM in this picture is the Type II model which has four circular windows in front and two behind. In the newer Type IV JIM, vision is improved by a completely clear plastic dome over the head.

Diver breathes through close fitting mask

JIM is lifted to and from the surface by this heavy cable. It also doubles as a telephone line.

JIM Type II's hull is made of hardened magnesium alloy. Glass reinforced plastic has replaced this for the Type IV.

JIM's mechanical hands, called manipulators, can pick up quite small objects.

The limb joints on JIM's arms and legs contain fluid which prevents them seizing up.

▲ Shown here is one of JIM's ancestors, made in 1715 by John Lethbridge. He reached a depth of 20 m during a dive in his wood and iron invention. The diver lay flat on his front looking out of a window, his arms poking out of two holes.

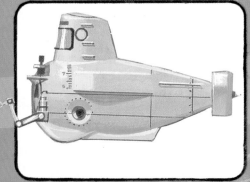

▲ Shown here is Alvin, a three-man submersible in which divers can work at great depths. The Alvin was one of the underwater vehicles used to film the *SS Titanic* when it was discovered in 1988.

esting water buoyancy

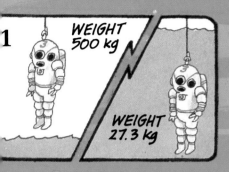

1
WEIGHT 500 kg

WEIGHT 27.3 kg

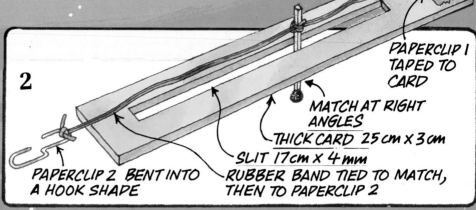

2
PAPERCLIP 1 TAPED TO CARD

MATCH AT RIGHT ANGLES

THICK CARD 25 cm x 3 cm

SLIT 17 cm x 4 mm

PAPERCLIP 2 BENT INTO A HOOK SHAPE

RUBBER BAND TIED TO MATCH, THEN TO PAPERCLIP 2

▲ This water buoyancy meter will let you measure the weight drop of objects in water. You need a bowl, plasticine, a used match, some thick card, three paperclips and a rubber band. Cut the rubber band in half to get a single length.

Cut out the card and assemble the meter as shown in the picture above. Make sure that the match pointer moves smoothly in the central slit. To add the weighing scale, first mark on the position at which the match points.

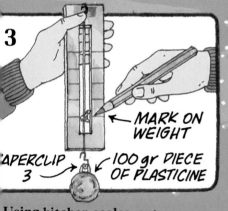

3
MARK ON WEIGHT

PAPERCLIP 3

100 gr PIECE OF PLASTICINE

Using kitchen scales, cut ur pieces of plasticine weighing 50, 75, and 100 g each. Hang em in turn from the meter's hook. ark on the scale where the match ints to with each different ece of plasticine.

4
DO NOT DROP METER IN !

▲ Hook the 100 gr piece of plasticine onto the meter. Check that the match pointer is against the 100 g mark on the scale. Fill the bowl with water, and lower the plasticine gently in. Its weight will drop to about 45 g.

5
25
50

▲ Salty water is even more buoyant than fresh. Try dissolving lots of salt in the bowl. The plasticine's weight will drop even more. When you have finished with the weight experiments, use the salty water for the corrosion experiment below.

orrosion underwater

1
SALTY WATER
TIN LIDS
NAILS

IM's magnesium hull is hardened resist corrosion from the sea, ich acts just like a weak acid. y this experiment using two ked-bean tin lids, two iron ls and the bowl of salty water m the buoyancy experiment

2

▲ Metals rust at different rates. Test this by putting a tin lid and a nail into the bowl of salt water. Make sure they do not touch. You will see that the nail starts to rust in a few hours, whereas the tin lid takes much longer.

3
NAIL AND LID TIED UP

▲ Galvanic corrosion is caused when different metals touch one another. Bind the other tin lid and nail together with cotton thread and put them in the water. You will see that the touching parts rust quicker than the rest.

Development of the submarine

The first submarine was invented in 1578 by an Englishman, William Bourne, but it had no means of propulsion. The Turtle, launched in 1776, was little better, using muscle powered propellers. The German U (Unterseeboote—undersea boat) boats used in World War I were the first major use of submarine power at war.

Since then, submarines have developed into the most important weapon in modern military arsenals. The picture on the right is typical of a present-day missile-carrying atomic-powered submarine. The details may change from type to type, but the general features are similar the world over. The whale-shaped hull is designed to operate most efficiently underwater.

David Bushnell's *Turt* **was armed with a 68 k gunpowder bomb and cruised underwater f about 30 minutes befo the pilot had to open the hatch for fresh ai**

The French *Gymnote* (*Eel*) **was launched in 1888. She was powered by electric motors and was armed with a torpedo in her bow. She was rebuilt 10 years later with a conning tower replacing the single periscope mast and twin torpedoes slung either side of it.**

Multi-bladed propeller —

Aft hydroplane —

Rudder —

Main motor room housing the propulsion turbines, which turn the propeller, and the turbo-generators, which supply electricity.

Aft escape tower. Four men at a time can escape through the aft and forward escape towers. If a diver needs to examine the outside of the hull, he leaves and returns by the escape tower.

1 Keeping control of a submarine

If a submarine is too buoyant it will stay on the surface like a ship. If its weight is increased it becomes less buoyant. At a certain weight it will submerge. To stay submerged without sinking or rising—to be neutrally buoyant—the submarine must weigh the same as the amount of water that it displaces. So, as fuel and stores (up to 2,500 tonnes of them) are used up, water is let into compensating tanks to make up the weight difference.

2

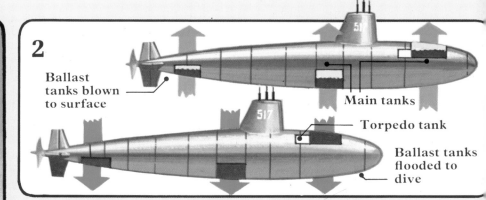

Ballast tanks blown to surface

Main tanks

Torpedo tank

Ballast tanks flooded to dive

▲ The main ballast tanks are the key to submerging and surfacing. On the surface, these tanks are filled with air. To submerge, they are both completely filled with water. To return to the surface, compressed air is forced into the tanks. This forces the water out, and the submarine rises to the surface.

After missiles or torpedoes have been fired, water is let into small torpedo tanks to compensate for the weight loss.

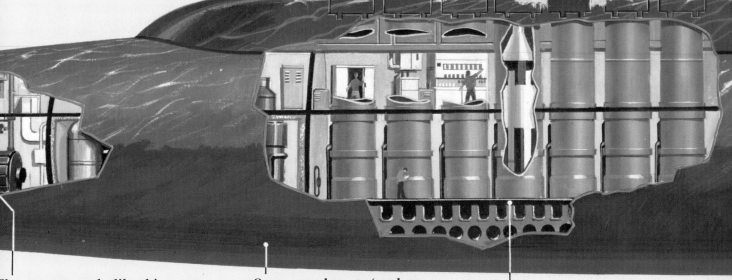

peed at sea is
sually measured
n knots. One knot
s equivalent to
.85kph (1.15mph).

Typical cruise speed
is around 45 kph
underwater, 36 kph
on the surface.

A typical warload is 16
Polaris missiles. Each has three
separate H-bomb warheads which
can be directed to different
targets far apart. The missiles
are blown out of their launch
tubes by compressed air. The missiles'
engines fire when they are
clear of the tube.

he cigar-shaped Holland submarine
as built for the US Navy and the
ritish Royal Navy. The Number 8
esign, shown here, was bought by
e US Navy in 1900. She was
quipped with a single torpedo and
uld cruise underwater at 9 kph.

The missile hatches are opened
just before the missiles are
fired.

The reactor works like this—water
s pumped around the radio-active
hot core and is turned into steam.
The steam spins turbines which
urn the propeller and
enerate electricity.

Sewage and waste (such as
potato peelings) are a
problem as disposal is difficult
at depth. They are normally
stored and pumped out
back at base.

Missile decks where the missiles
are prepared for firing, and minor
servicing undertaken.

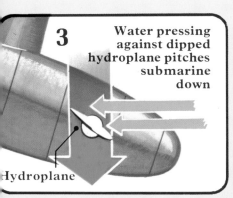

3 Water pressing
against dipped
hydroplane pitches
submarine
down

Hydroplane

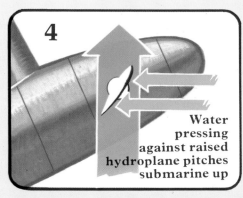

4 Water
pressing
against raised
hydroplane pitches
submarine up

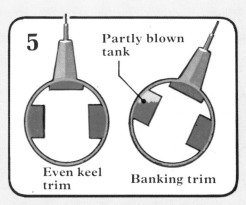

5 Partly blown
tank

Even keel
trim

Banking trim

▲ Underwater, hydroplanes control
he angle of the submarine. To
ive, the forward hydroplanes are
ipped, the aft pair raised. As
he submarine moves along, water
ressing against the tops of the
orward hydroplanes forces the bows

down (above left), water pressing
against the bottoms of the aft
hydroplanes forces the stern up.
The submarine then cruises down at
the dipped angle, its tanks flooded
to make it sink. To surface, this
sequence is reversed (above right).

▲ Special trimming tanks help to
keep the submarine stable as it
changes course. If the craft
turns to starboard (to the right),
water is blown from the port (left)
tank to bank the submarine into
the 'corner'.

On top of the fin (called the sail in the US Navy) are the search and attack periscopes, radio antennae, and the snort induction mast. This sucks in air if the submarine is not running on its reactor and has come close to the surface to recharge its batteries.

In the missile control centre the missiles are given their target instructions and, if necessary, fired.

The control room is the nerve centre of the ship.

Wardroom where the submarine's officers eat and relax.

The wireless office receives messages and orders. It never transmits—to do so would give the submarine's position away.

The navigation centre where the submarine's course is plotted and checked.

The sound room. The sonar team can locate nearby ships and submarines using a sound analysing system.

Make your own periscope

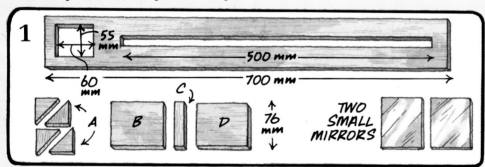

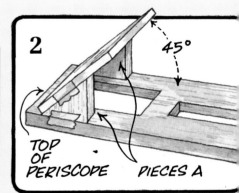

▲ This periscope, though not designed for underwater work, will enable you to spy over walls and see around corners. You need two small hand mirrors, which you can get from the cosmetics department of a large store. You also need sticky tape, balsa glue, 6 mm thick balsa wood, and some transparent acetate. Cut out the balsa wood to the sizes and shapes shown in the plans above. An easy way to cut a 45° triangle is to cut a square in half from corner to corner.

▲ The square hole for the top mirror should be a little smaller than the mirror itself, so its size will vary depending on the size of your mirror. Tape a mirror to two triangle struts, then tape the assembly in place as shown.

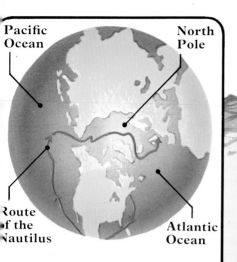

Pacific Ocean
North Pole
Route of the Nautilus
Atlantic Ocean

At 11.15 on August 3, 1958 Commander Anderson took the atomic submarine *USS Nautilus* under the North Pole.

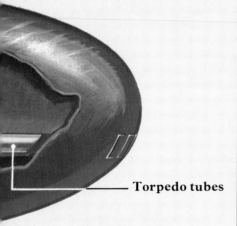

Torpedo tubes

Each torpedo is powered by its own electric motor and can be guided onto its target after it has been fired. It creates neither wake nor noise, either of which might reveal the submarine's position.

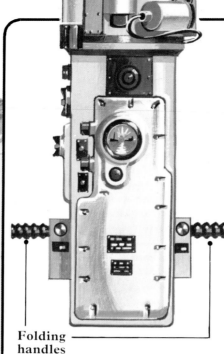

Folding handles

A periscope is one of the ways a submarine can discover what is happening on the surface and in the sky while remaining submerged. Most submarines have two—the search and the attack periscopes. The search periscope is for normal use. It can easily be seen, so the attack periscope, which is slim and difficult to spot, is used if the submarine is attacking enemy craft.

Most periscopes have an image-intensifier. This aids visibility in poor weather, by amplifying the picture, rather like turning up the brightness on a television screen. Periscopes also have range-finders to calculate how far away a target is.

Commander's eye-view of the sea

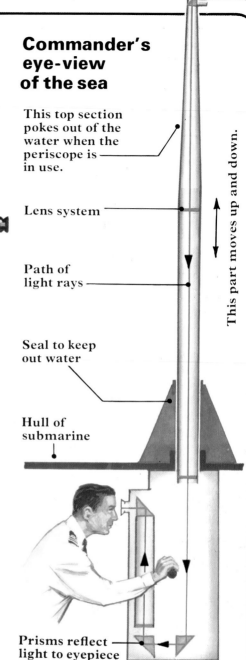

This top section pokes out of the water when the periscope is in use.

Lens system

Path of light rays

Seal to keep out water

Hull of submarine

Prisms reflect light to eyepiece

This part moves up and down.

3

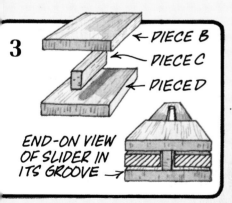

PIECE B
PIECE C
PIECE D

END-ON VIEW OF SLIDER IN ITS GROOVE

▲ The H-shaped slider moves in the central slot. Assemble the three parts of it together with glue, making sure they can move freely up and down. Hold the parts together with pins until they have dried thoroughly.

4

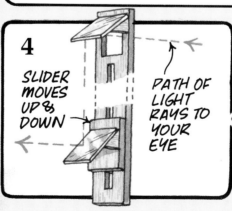

SLIDER MOVES UP & DOWN

PATH OF LIGHT RAYS TO YOUR EYE

▲ Glue and tape the other two triangle struts onto the slider, then tape the mirror in place as the picture above shows. The dotted red line shows the path light rays take on their way from the target to your eye.

5

TAPE

▲ Draw sights on a piece of acetate (or any clear plastic) and tape it in front of the square hole. To use, hold the slider to your eye with your left hand. Move the main body of the periscope up and down with your right hand.

Mammals of the sea

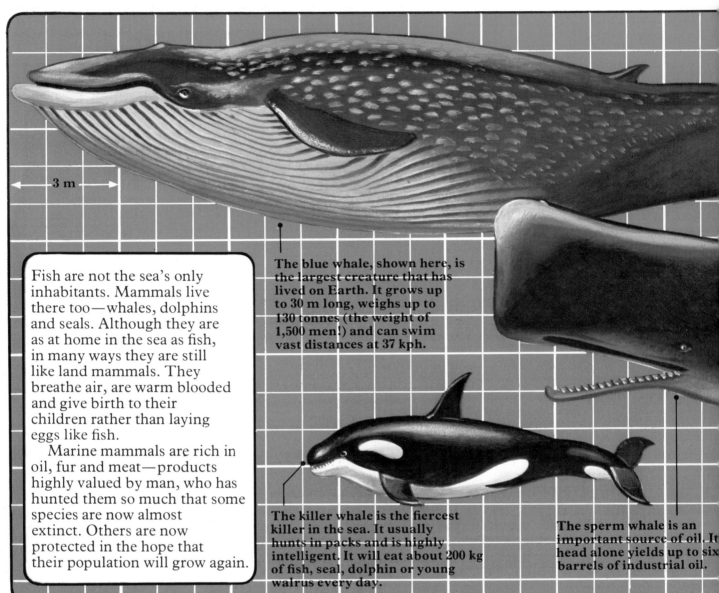

3 m

Fish are not the sea's only inhabitants. Mammals live there too—whales, dolphins and seals. Although they are as at home in the sea as fish, in many ways they are still like land mammals. They breathe air, are warm blooded and give birth to their children rather than laying eggs like fish.

Marine mammals are rich in oil, fur and meat—products highly valued by man, who has hunted them so much that some species are now almost extinct. Others are now protected in the hope that their population will grow again.

The blue whale, shown here, is the largest creature that has lived on Earth. It grows up to 30 m long, weighs up to 130 tonnes (the weight of 1,500 men!) and can swim vast distances at 37 kph.

The killer whale is the fiercest killer in the sea. It usually hunts in packs and is highly intelligent. It will eat about 200 kg of fish, seal, dolphin or young walrus every day.

The sperm whale is an important source of oil. It head alone yields up to six barrels of industrial oil.

Two types of whale . . .

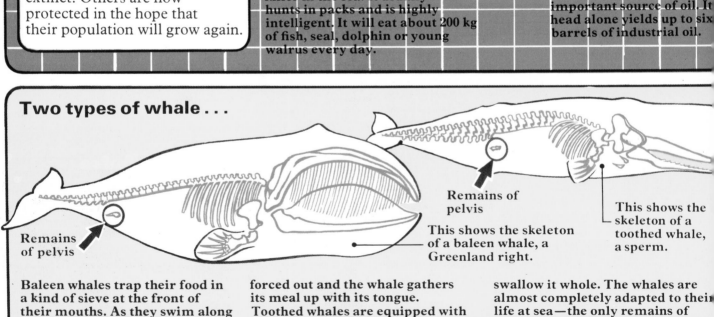

Remains of pelvis

Remains of pelvis

This shows the skeleton of a baleen whale, a Greenland right.

This shows the skeleton of a toothed whale, a sperm.

Baleen whales trap their food in a kind of sieve at the front of their mouths. As they swim along openmouthed, water flows in and food is caught in the strands of baleen. The water is then forced out and the whale gathers its meal up with its tongue. Toothed whales are equipped with 60 teeth, each one about 200 mm long and weighing around 3 kg. They do not chew their food, but swallow it whole. The whales are almost completely adapted to their life at sea—the only remains of their pelvis for example, is the tiny bone structure arrowed in the skeletons shown above.

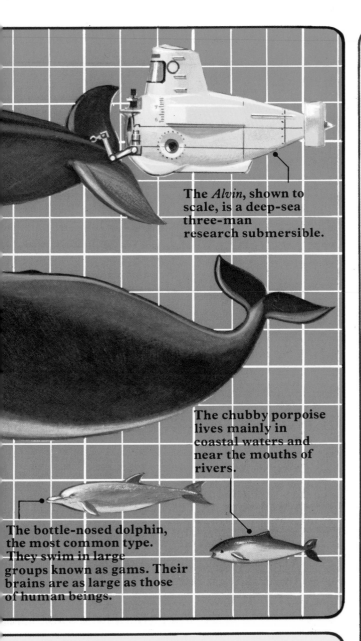

The *Alvin*, shown to scale, is a deep-sea three-man research submersible.

The chubby porpoise lives mainly in coastal waters and near the mouths of rivers.

The bottle-nosed dolphin, the most common type. They swim in large groups known as gams. Their brains are as large as those of human beings.

. . . and their menu for lunch

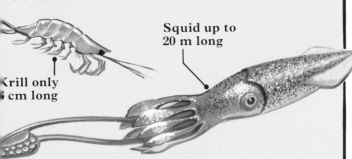

Squid up to 20 m long

Krill only 6 cm long

Baleen whales live on krill, a small shrimp-like plankton creature. Sperm whales live mainly on squid, which are more difficult to capture than krill. Sucker-scars have been found on whales showing that they have fought giant squids up to 20 m long.

Dolphins—marvels of nature's engineering

Hungry dolphins use an echo-reflecting system to find their prey. They make very high pitched clicks in their nose passages, sending them out as concentrated beams of sound waves. The sound waves reflect off anything in their way, the dolphin hears the echoes and 'homes-in' on the unfortunate fish.

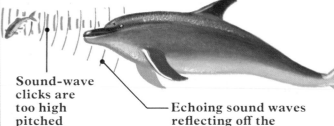

Sound-wave clicks are too high pitched for humans to hear.

Echoing sound waves reflecting off the prey are heard by the dolphin.

▼ Dolphin skin is fixed into long internal grooves, like inside-out fingerprints. They keep the skin taut and firm, cutting down the drag—the slowing down effect—of the water. The skin wobbles as it speeds along, constantly adjusting to eddies and turbulence, cutting down drag even more.

The underskin grooves exactly follow the line water takes as it flows around the body.

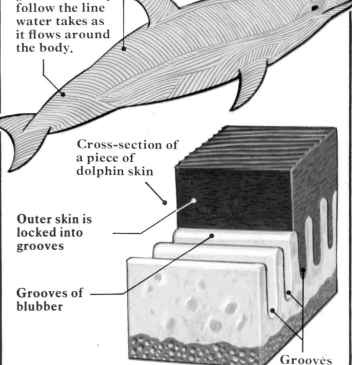

Cross-section of a piece of dolphin skin

Outer skin is locked into grooves

Grooves of blubber

Grooves

In the abyss

The struggle to survive in the cold and pitch black abyss is intense. Few fish live there because food is so short. Those that do tend to be small and their bodies are built to hunt for food. Many have tiny lights which shine out to lure their prey. Their mouths and stomachs are very flexible too, so they can attack and swallow up other fish that are sometimes bigger than themselves.

▲ The first deep-sea explorations were made by Barton and Beebe, two American scientists. In 1934 they went down to 923 m in their bathysphere, shown above, a record depth that was only exceeded 15 years later.

Ugly faces of the deep

Large-mouthed and ugly tends to be the general rule in the deeps. Here are just five examples of deep-sea dwellers.

As her name implies, this female angler fish goes fishing for food. Her bait is the lighted tip of an extended ray that grows from her head.

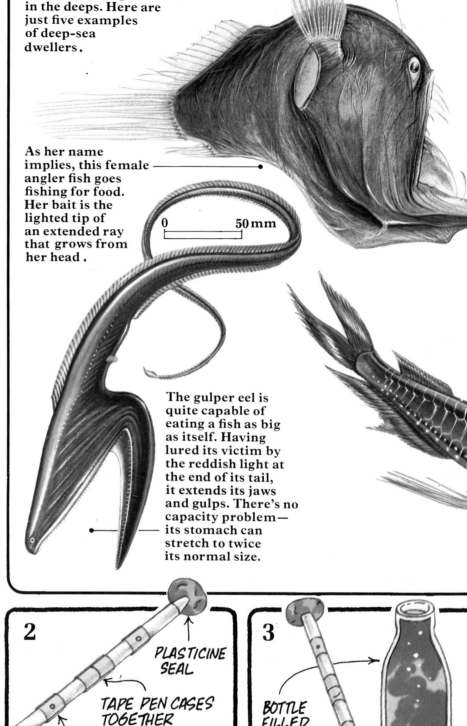

0   50 m

0   50 mm

The gulper eel is quite capable of eating a fish as big as itself. Having lured its victim by the reddish light at the end of its tail, it extends its jaws and gulps. There's no capacity problem— its stomach can stretch to twice its normal size.

The weight of water

1

TAPE

PLASTICINE

EMPTY BALLPOINT PEN CASES

2

PLASTICINE SEAL

TAPE PEN CASES TOGETHER

SEAL BREATHER HOLES

3

BOTTLE FILLED WITH WATER

▲ This experiment shows you how water pressure works at a depth, even though you only need to dive to the bottom of a bottle. You need two empty ballpoint pen cases, some plasticine and a roll of waterproof sticky tape.

▲ Tape the two pen cases together ends-on as shown above. Make sure you tape up the small 'breather' holes half-way up each case. Use the plasticine to seal one end of the long tube you have made. Blow down the tube to check the seals.

▲ Fill up a milk bottle (or any other tall glass jar) with water. Plunge the tube, open end down, to the bottom of the jar. You should see the surrounding water press a little way, about 10 mm, up into the tube.

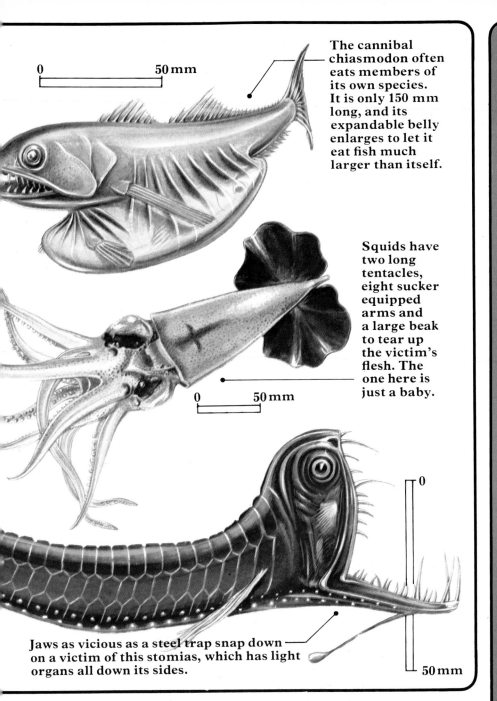

0   50 mm

The cannibal chiasmodon often eats members of its own species. It is only 150 mm long, and its expandable belly enlarges to let it eat fish much larger than itself.

Squids have two long tentacles, eight sucker equipped arms and a large beak to tear up the victim's flesh. The one here is just a baby.

0   50 mm

0

50 mm

Jaws as vicious as a steel trap snap down on a victim of this stomias, which has light organs all down its sides.

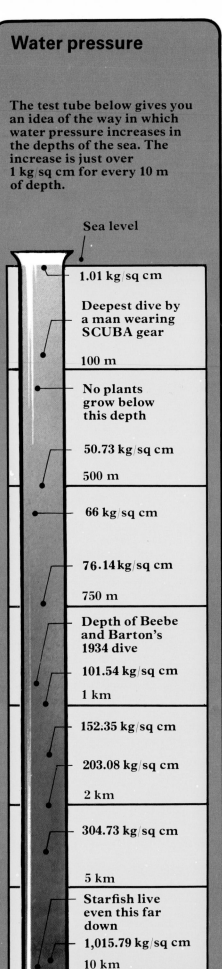

The test tube below gives you an idea of the way in which water pressure increases in the depths of the sea. The increase is just over 1 kg/sq cm for every 10 m of depth.

Sea level

1.01 kg/sq cm

Deepest dive by a man wearing SCUBA gear

100 m

No plants grow below this depth

50.73 kg/sq cm

500 m

66 kg/sq cm

76.14 kg/sq cm

750 m

Depth of Beebe and Barton's 1934 dive

101.54 kg/sq cm

1 km

152.35 kg/sq cm

203.08 kg/sq cm

2 km

304.73 kg/sq cm

5 km

Starfish live even this far down

1,015.79 kg/sq cm

10 km

4

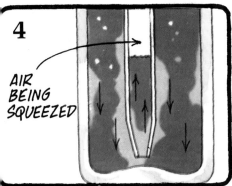

AIR BEING SQUEEZED

▲ The water is squeezing the air in the tube. The deeper you go, the more the increasing water pressure will squash the trapped air. Move the tube quickly up and down to see how the effect of the water pressure varies with depth.

5

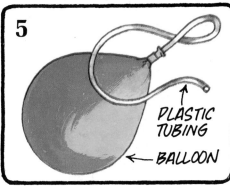

PLASTIC TUBING

BALLOON

▲ Try blowing up a balloon tied to a plastic or rubber tube. It is quite easy to do in air, but with the balloon at the bottom of a water-filled sink, it is next to impossible because of the water pressing in on the balloon.

Ocean harvest

For thousands of years the oceans have been a rich source of food. Now they are also an important source of energy, since oil and gas have been discovered under the seabed.

Many of the resources of the seas are in danger of being spoilt by man. Pollution not only directly harms seabirds and fish but also enters the food pyramid, causing enormous damage to the whole of ocean life.

Overfishing has reduced the size of fish stocks in some areas because too many young fish have been caught before they can breed.

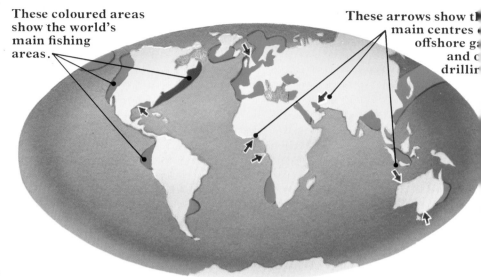

These coloured areas show the world's main fishing areas.

These arrows show t main centres offshore g and d drillir

Purse seine and Otter trawl

The purse seine is used to encircle schools of fish such as tuna. Once the fish are surrounded, the net is drawn together and hauled up. Trawls are dragged along the seabed, frightening bottom-dwelling fish such as sole into the net.

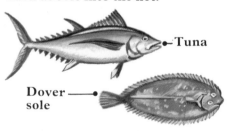

Tuna

Dover sole

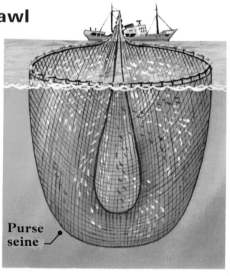

Purse seine

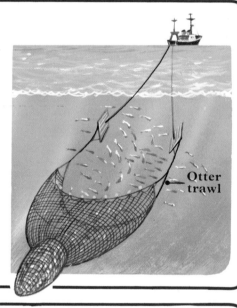

Otter trawl

Drift net

Drift nets trap herring and mackerel when they come to the surface at night to feed on plankton. The nets are stretched across the water, suspended from air-filled floats, and trap the fish as they try to swim through.

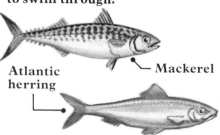

Atlantic herring

Mackerel

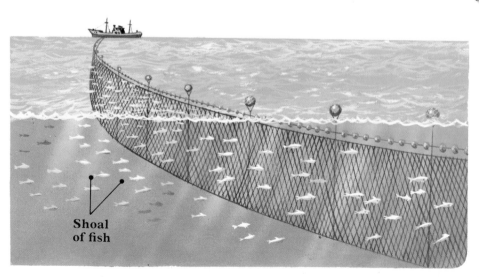

Shoal of fish

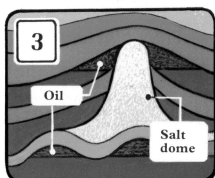

Black gold under the sea

Geologists think oil was formed like this. Millions of years ago the dead remains of sea-dwelling plants and animals sank to the seabed. As time went by, many layers of sediment collected on top, each layer compressing the ones under it. Increasing pressure and heat crushed the dead remains together and they turned, by a process not fully understood, into oil. Oil fields consist of two types of rock. Porous reservoir rock, saturated with oil, and cap rock which lies on top of the reservoir rock. Oil cannot penetrate it, remaining trapped in the reservoir rock underneath.

Big twin-engined Sikorsky S-61 helicopter

A rig like this one needs about 70 crewmen to keep it operating 24 hours a day.

Support craft brings water and supplies to the drilling rig

This type of oil rig is firmly fixed into the sea bed. For deeper water drilling floating rigs are used, held in place by cables anchored to the sea floor.

Well-head

Drill pipe through which the drilling bit is lowered

The rotary drill bit

The essential tool in drilling for oil is the rotary drill bit. Its large metal teeth can grind their way through virtually any rock—though the harder the rock, the longer it takes and the more frequently it has to be changed.

Oil traps

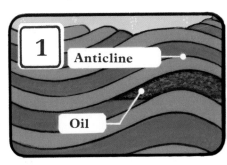

1 Anticline

Oil

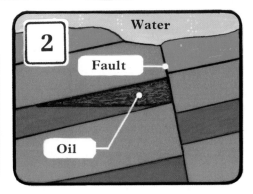

2 Water

Fault

Oil

3

Oil

Salt dome

▲ When geologists hunt for oil, they try to find special rock formations where oil deposits are likely to be trapped. Three of these formations are shown in the diagrams above. An anticline (1), is a fold of rock. Oil can be

trapped at the top of the fold. In a fault (2), oil can be trapped behind a wedge of cap rock which has slipped down into the reservoir rock. Another trap occurs when a rock salt dome (3), forces its way upwards, bending the reservoir

rock into arches and sealing it off with a layer of salt. Oil is trapped in the reservoir rock rather like water in a wet sponge. Have a look at one next time you have a bath to see the effect.

Inner space

Inner space is the name given to the new frontier under the sea. More people and more demand for raw materials for industry mean that the sea is growing in importance as a source of supply for food and minerals.

The difficult problem is to devise ways of using the seas' resources, whilst controlling pollution and conserving fish stocks.

A few ideas of the scenes you might see if you went on an underwater trip in the future are shown on these two pages.

▲ This picture shows the sort of undersea city that may be built in the future, perched right on the edge of a continental shelf. The globular 'people-pods' shown in this design are built on steel legs with entry hatches on their undersides. They are pressurized and provide the diving community with all the comforts of life on land. Schools, libraries and theatres are just a few of the things inside the warm air-conditioned spheres.

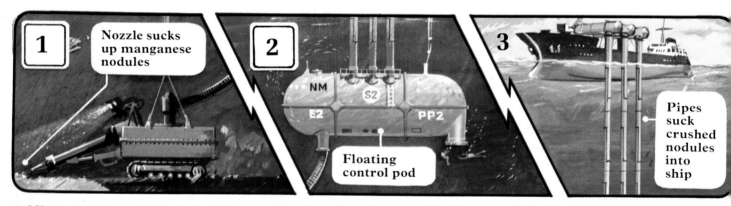

1 Nozzle sucks up manganese nodules

2 Floating control pod

3 Pipes suck crushed nodules into ship

▲ Mineral mining will be one of the most important developments in the future. The pictures above show a design for harvesting manganese nodules, which lie scattered over the world's seabeds. Manganese nodules look like jagged lumps 2–30 cm across and contain other minerals as well, such as nickel, copper, cobalt and lead. The picture sequence shows a robot crawler (1) sucking up nodules with its vacuum cleaner nose-probe. They are piped to a floating control pod (2) where they are ground up into a fine powder. The powder is sucked up by powerful pumps into the hold of a waiting cargo ship (3) on the ocean surface far above.

Underwater fish farm

This picture shows a two-seat sea scooter (1) nearing a fish farm cage (2). The cage 'walls' are made of bubbles leaked from a compressed-air pipe system on the sea-bed. Fish can be kept like this because they do not like passing through the bubble walls. Trained dolphins (3) help the fish farmers tend the cages. On the right, divers poke the suction hose of a fishing boat (4) into a cage. Fish are then simply sucked up and into the ship's hold to be fresh-frozen.

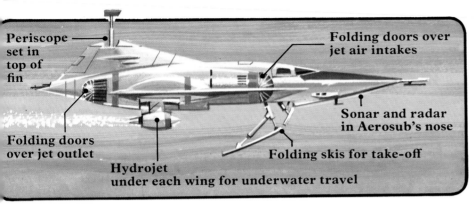

Periscope set in top of fin

Folding doors over jet air intakes

Folding doors over jet outlet

Hydrojet under each wing for underwater travel

Folding skis for take-off

Sonar and radar in Aerosub's nose

Military developments will be an important part of tomorrow's world. One new idea is shown above—the flying submarine. The Aerosub would fly to within a few hundred miles of its target, then dive down into the water to hide from the enemy's radar. It would carry on underwater, only emerging when near the target. It would then accelerate to supersonic speeds for the final part of its mission.

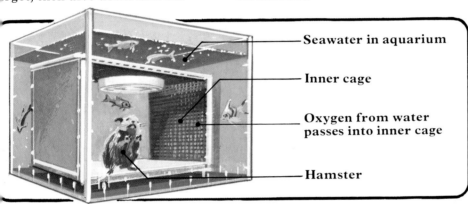

Seawater in aquarium

Inner cage

Oxygen from water passes into inner cage

Hamster

Scientists are already trying to develop artificial gills and the picture above shows one type they are experimenting with. The hamster is in a rubber-walled cage. The rubber, called neoprene, allows the oxygen of the water in the outer cage to pass through it. Enough oxygen percolates through for the hamster to breathe easily. Miniaturized versions of this system would be ideal for the 21st century diver.

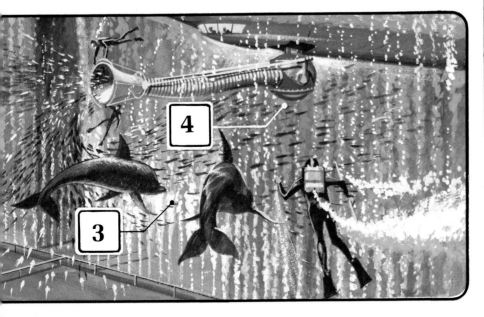

Water power

The core of this design for a pollution-free power station is a tank of ammonia. Ammonia only needs a very small temperature difference to change from liquid to gas and back again.

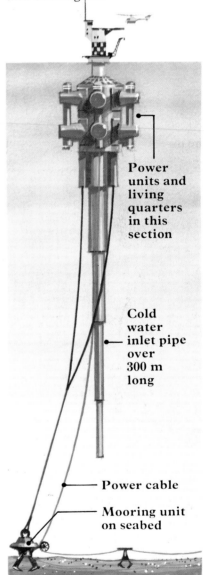

Power units and living quarters in this section

Cold water inlet pipe over 300 m long

Power cable

Mooring unit on seabed

Warm, surface water is pumped around the ammonia tank. The ammonia turns into gas and is used to spin turbines which generate electricity. Cold, bottom water is pumped up the inlet pipe to turn the gas back into a liquid again. The cycle continues indefinitely, generating electricity 24 hours a day.

Undersea firsts

Stories of men's exploits undersea go back to ancient legends. The first account that seems reasonably certain is of a father and daughter team of divers, Scyllias and Cyana, who successfully recovered valuables from a sunken ship for King Xerxes of Persia in about 450 BC.

These are some of the other firsts in the history of the undersea.

323 BC
A diving bell was used by Alexander the Great to examine the underwater defences of Tyre, a stronghold on the shores of what is now the Lebanon.

1624
Cornelius van Drebbel, a Dutchman living in England, launched the first 'submarine' on the Thames. In fact, it was more like a half-submerged rowing boat.

1819
The first standard 'open' diving suit was perfected by a German, Augustus Siebe, but water could leak in if the diver bent over or moved too quickly.

1837
Siebe produced the first totally sealed 'closed' diving suit, far safer than the open version. Its basic design is still in use today.

1896
The first off-shore oil well was drilled off the coast of California, USA.

1930
Barton and Beebe made the first test-dive in their bathysphere.

1955
The first nuclear submarine, *USS Nautilus*, was completed.

1962
As an experiment in living under the sea, Jacques Cousteau began the first of his Continental Shelf Station (Conshelf) projects. In it, two men spent just over a week 10m down off Marseilles in Southern France.

1981
An Anglo-Russian expedition located the wreck of *HMS Edinburgh* which sank in the Second World War. They salvaged hundreds of gold bars which had been part of her cargo.

1982
Henry VIII's flagship, the *Mary Rose* which sank in the Solent was lifted to the surface following an underwater archaeological dig. This was led by the diver and archaeologist, Margaret Rule.

1988
An expedition led by Russ Ballard located and filmed the *SS Titanic* which sank in 1911. It lies on the seabed two miles down in the Atlantic.

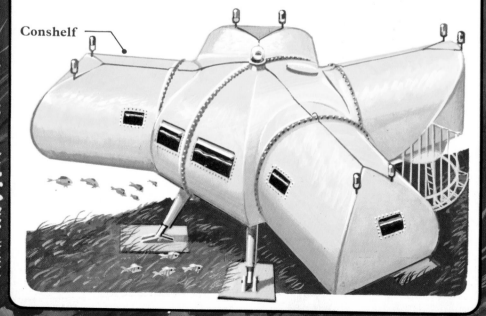

Conshelf

Undersea facts

Water makes life possible. Without it, neither people nor animals could live, and the Earth would be uninhabitable. This is the most important fact of all about the sea – that it gives us life and that life started there. But there are lots of other fascinating facts about the oceans and the creatures that live there. Here are just a few of them.

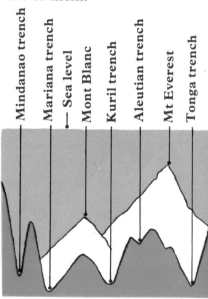

Mindanao trench · Mariana trench · Sea level · Mont Blanc · Kuril trench · Aleutian trench · Mt Everest · Tonga trench

The diagram above shows some of the deepest trenches in the oceans. The world's highest mountain, Mount Everest (8,848 m) and the highest peak in the Alps, Mont Blanc (4,800 m) are quite small in comparison.

Over 97 per cent of all the world's water is stored in the oceans. They hold 1,373 million cubic km of water spread out over 356 million square km.

The fastest swimmers in the ocean are marlin and sailfish, both of which can reach speeds of 80 kph. Flying fish move at 56 kph as they take off.

Tuna fish rarely stop swimming and usually move along at a steady 15 kph. By the time it is fifteen years old, a tuna will have travelled more than 1.6 million km.

The record for an undersea stay held by four scientists who took part in Operation Tektite off the Virgin Islands in 1968. They spent 60 days in a pressurized laboratory at a depth of 15 m.

The most endangered dolphin is the Chinese river dolphin. There may be as few as 200 left. This is because the river in which they live is constantly being fished and is polluted with sewerage.

The manganese nodules scattered on the floor of the Pacific Ocean contain enough aluminium to supply man's needs for about 20,000 years, enough copper for 6,000 years and enough manganese for no less than 400,000 years.

The wobbegong is the 'black sheep' of the shark family. First, it doesn't have to keep moving in order to breathe, unlike other sharks. Second, it uses cunning, not speed, to trap its food. Since it looks rather like a rock overgrown with seaweed, all it needs to do is to lie on the ocean bottom and snap up its victims as they swim unsuspectingly by.

The coelacanth, shown below, is a living fossil of the sea. Its appearance has hardly changed for over 350 million years. It was thought to have become extinct more than 70 million years ago, but in 1938 one was caught by fishermen off the mouth of the Chalumna River in South East Africa.

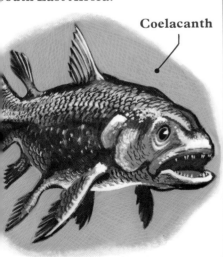

Coelacanth

Undersea words

This list of words only covers terms not fully explained elsewhere in this book. You will find some of the words to do with fishes explained on pages 8 and 9.

Continental slope

Continental shelf

Abyssal plain

Bathysphere
Kind of diving bell, shaped like a globe, used for observing the undersea. Winched down on a cable from its support ship.

Bends
Pains suffered by a diver in his joints and muscles as a result of surfacing too quickly. So-called because divers tend to twist and bend their bodies in an attempt to relieve the pain. Its scientific name is caisson sickness.

Continental shelf
The relatively shallow area of the seabed that surrounds most land masses. It is usually no more than 200 m deep but extends for widely varying distances from the coast.

Continental slope
The steeper slope down from the end of the continental shelf towards the ocean bed.

Decompression
The reduction of pressure in the body as a diver goes up toward the surface. Usually carried out by stopping from time to time on the way up or in an underwater decompression chamber.

Habitat
The place in which a plant or animal lives.

Lateral line
Pressure sensitive line running along a fish's body, from just behind the gills to the base of the tail fin. It can detect other fish or object nearby

Mollusc
Soft-bodied creature with no backbone. Most molluscs have hard shells, such as oysters. They all have a single foot, but that of, for example, the octopus is divided into eight tentacles.

Plankton
Small organisms drifting in the upper parts of the oceans. Phyto-plankton are plants, zooplankton are animals.

Snort
The snort mast enables a conventional submarine to recharge its batteries and to renew its air supply by running its engines while still submerged. Only the top of the snort induction mast—down which the engines suck air—appears above the surface of the sea.

Sonar
Detection device in ships and submarines. It sends out a sound beam and receives the echo which bounces off other objects in the sea. The distance of the object is worked out by the time gap between the sound pulse sent out and the echo received. Sound travels at 3,600 kph underwater, so a two second delay between the beam being sent out and its echo being received, means that the object is about 1 km away.

Index

Going further

Places to visit

There are a number of ways in which you can follow up your interest in the Undersea.

If you are keen on studying underwater technology, visit science, naval and maritime museums.

If the animal life of the sea is your main interest, an aquarium is the place to see it at first hand. Some seaside towns have sealife centres which house a range of aquariums showing examples of local sealife.

If you can swim well, the most exciting way to get to know the Undersea is to go diving. Try to find a club where you can learn to snorkel dive and move on to SCUBA diving when you are fourteen. But – diving is dangerous. Don't attempt it except under the supervision of a qualified adult.

Books to read

Encyclopaedia of Underwater Life
by Banister and Campbell
Allen and Unwin, 1985

Usborne Mysteries and Marvels of Ocean Life
by Rick Morris
Usborne, 1983

Guide to the Seashore and Shallow Seas
by A C Campbell
Hamlyn, 1989

The Living Sea
by Jacques Cousteau
Hamish Hamilton, 1988